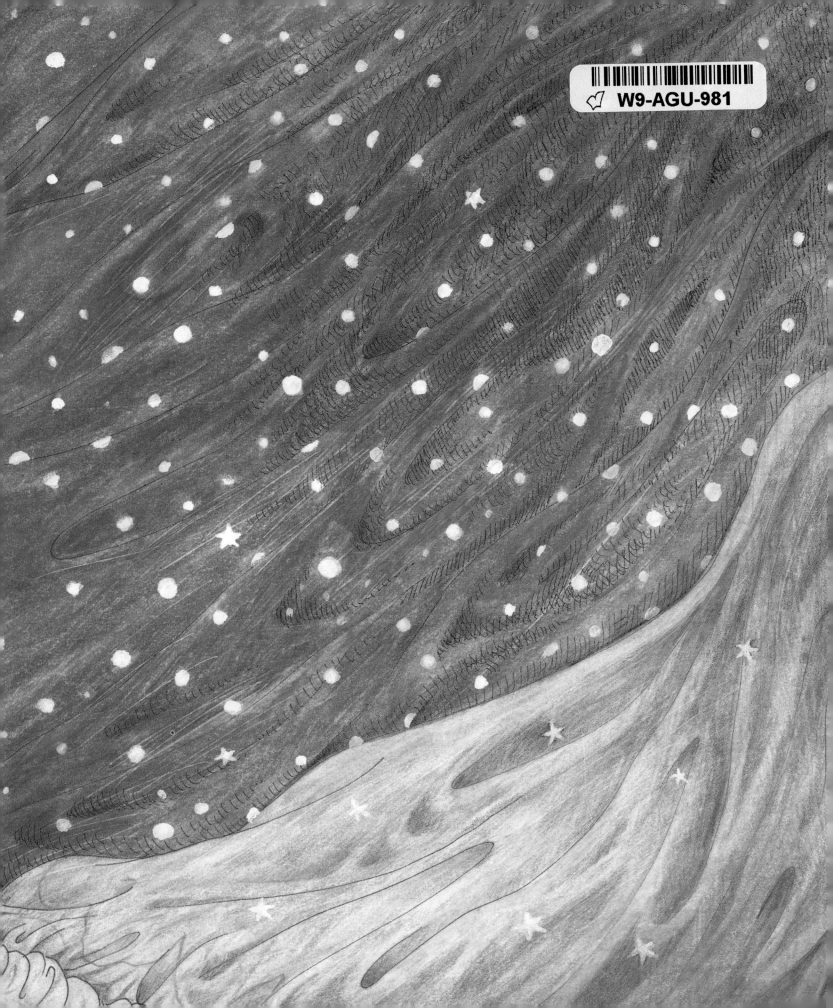

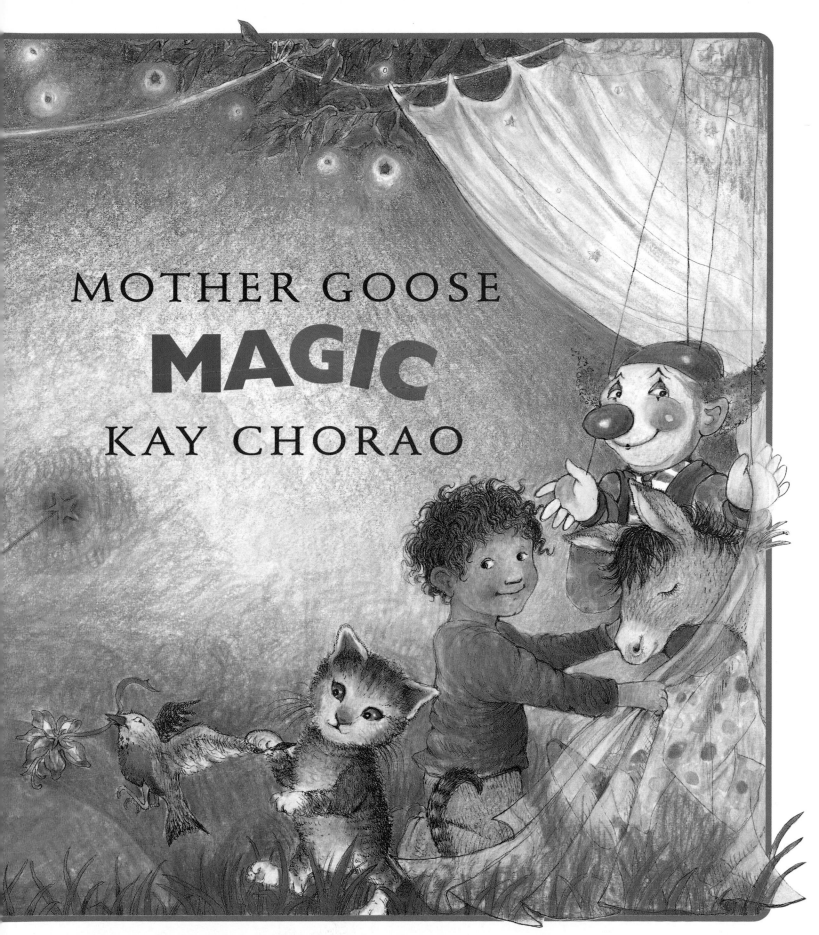

MOTHER GOOSE
MAGIC
KAY CHORAO

DUTTON CHILDREN'S BOOKS · NEW YORK

Library of Congress Cataloging-in-Publication Data
Chorao, Kay.
Mother Goose magic/Kay Chorao.—1st ed.
p. cm.
Contents: Donkey, donkey—Dickory, dickory, dare—Little Robin
Red Breast—Sam, Sam, the butcher man—I like little pussy—
Joshua Lane—Jumping and tumbling—Nanny Button Cap.
ISBN 0-525-45064-5
1. Nursery rhymes. 2. Children's poetry. [1. Nursery rhymes.]
I. Title.
PZ8.3.C454Mo 1994
398.8—dc20   92-37160 CIP AC

Published in the United States 1994 by
Dutton Children's Books,
a division of Penguin Books USA Inc.
375 Hudson Street, New York, New York 10014

Designed by Riki Levinson

Printed in Hong Kong by South China Printing Co.
First edition   10 9 8 7 6 5 4 3 2 1

Contents

Donkey, Donkey   6

Dickory, Dickory, Dare   12

Little Robin Red Breast   21

Sam, Sam, the Butcher Man   25

I Like Little Pussy   36

Joshua Lane   47

Jumping and Tumbling   54

Nanny Button Cap   60

Donkey, Donkey

Donkey, donkey, old and gray,
Ope your mouth, and gently bray;

Lift your ears

and blow your horn,

To wake the world this sleepy morn.

Dickory, Dickory, Dare

Dickory, dickory, dare.
The pig flew up in the air;

13

The man in brown

soon brought him . . .

DOWN!

Dickory, dickory,

dare.

Little Robin Red Breast

Little Robin Red Breast sat upon a rail,

Needle, naddle, went his head,

Wiggle, waggle, went his tail.

Sam, Sam, the Butcher Man

Sam, Sam, the butcher man,

Washed his face in a frying pan,

Combed his hair with a wagon wheel,

And . . .

died with a toothache in his heel.

Sam, Sam,

the butcher man.

I like little pussy,
Her coat is so warm,

And if I don't hurt her
She'll do me no harm.

So I'll not pull her tail,

Nor drive her away,

But Pussy and I

very gently will . . .

PLAY!

"I know I have lost my train,"
Said a man named Joshua Lane;

"But I'll run on the rails

With my coattails for sails

And maybe I'll catch it . . .

AGAIN!"

Jumping and Tumbling

In jumping and tumbling
We spend the whole day,

Till night by arriving

Has finished our play.

What then? One and all,
There's no more to be said,

As we tumbled all day,
So we tumble to bed.

Nanny Button Cap

The moon shines bright,
The stars give light.

And little Nanny Button Cap
Will come tomorrow night.